The Very Long Sausage Dog

Kristina Murray-Hally
Illustrated by Hanlik Arts

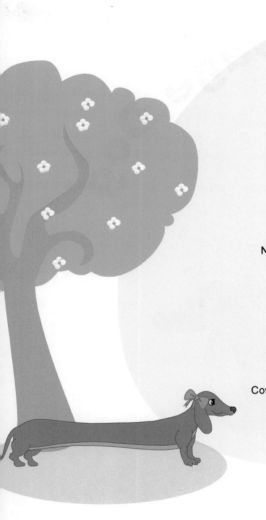

To Theadora and Seraphina
may you always see the incredible!

First published in Australia by
Spiders 8 Media
Postal: PO BOX 2379 Ivanhoe East VIC 3079
Email: murrayhally@gmail.com
Website: www.kristinamurray-hally.com

National Library of Australia Cataloguing-in-Publication entry

Creator: Murray-Hally, Kristina, author.
Title: The Very Long Sausage Dog / Kristina Murray-Hally;
illustrated by Hanlik Arts.

ISBN: 978-0-6487072-6-4 (paperback)
ISBN: 978-0-9942738-6-4 (hardback)
ISBN: 978-0-9942738-7-1 (epub)

Cover design by graphic designer Hanlik Arts & Willy Tanuwijaya

Printed by Ingram Spark

Rosie Thornbury loves her dog Sprinkles, who is quite a rascal.

Sometimes she refuses to go for a walk. Other times she turns her nose up at her dinner. Sprinkles really has a mind of her own.

One day while Rosie was at school, Sprinkles munched through their vegetable patch, chewed on the clothes that were hanging on the line, gnawed the garden hose and drank the milk that belonged to Miffy, the cat from next door.

On Rosie's way home from school she wondered if Sprinkles fancied a walk.

After having a snack and not realising what mischief Sprinkles had been up to, Rosie called, "Sprinkles! Time for your walk." Asleep on her bed, Sprinkles opened one eye then closed it.

Sprinkles decided to listen and she slowly stretched and moved her front legs.

Rosie put on her lead and off they went.

This is strange, thought Rosie as they passed the neighbours house and Mr and Mrs Duffy pointed at them.

This is strange, thought Rosie as they passed the bakery and the staff ran to the door and laughed.

This is strange, thought Rosie as her friend Daisy's eyebrows rose and her jaw dropped as she let go of her bag of apples.

As Sprinkles walked through the back gate at her usual leisurely pace, then up the steps and toward her bed, Rosie noticed that Sprinkles back legs were still around the corner!

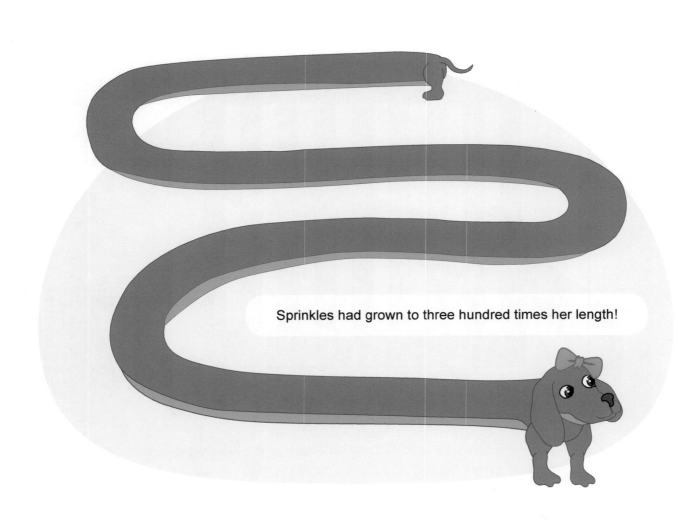

Sprinkles had grown to three hundred times her length!

"I'll call the vet," was all her mother said.

"Mum!" screamed Rosie. Rosie's mum came running, and as her gaze settled on Sprinkles, her eyes bulged and her mouth dropped open like a crocodile about to eat its prey.

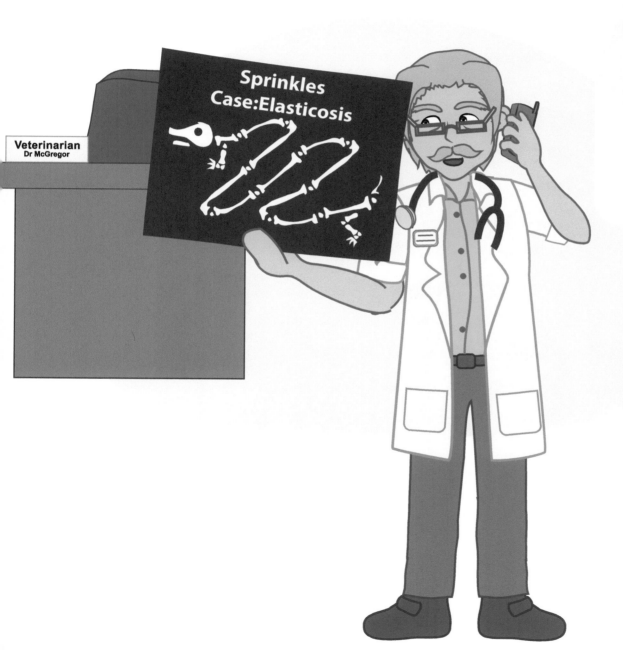

Later that evening, Dr McGregor rang. "She is showing the exact symptoms of Elasticosis, a rare condition caused by eating foreign material, and a build-up of wind," he explained.

"Start her on a special diet of prune juice
and bran dog biscuits,"
said Dr McGregor.
"She's fussy!" Rosie's mum replied.
"Disguise it or give her a reward!"
Dr McGregor replied.

There was no change. "Rosie, please help me get Sprinkles into the car," said her mum.

"Mrs Thornbury all I can tell you is
that you have a very special dog.
Celebrate her uniqueness!"
said Dr McGregor with a smile.

Sprinkles became a celebrity! She is still loveable and cheeky, just longer! And when Rosie takes her for a walk now, it takes a very long time.

NEWS

World Record Longest Dog

Acknowledgements

The Very Long Sausage Dog, Sprinkles and her family have been part of our family for some time and it is wonderful to be able to share this gorgeous story with you.

This book, as with my other creations have been a result of a great amount of work and my wonderful team.

Many thanks go to Hanlik Arts for his fantastic designs and amazing artwork. He is a great artist, fabulous to work with and crucial in the creation of this book.

It is with much gratitude that we say thank you to Willy Tanuwijaya for his wonderful work with the typesetting and layout of this book. Willy and Hanlik Arts are a fabulous team who work so well together.

Another grand thank you is for Amanda Spedding for her great editing and proofreading skills, her dedication and timely work, attention to detail, ideas and feedback.

An enormous thank you goes to our beautiful daughters, Theadora and Seraphina, my true inspiration.

Also a gigantic thank you goes to my husband, Tony, for his generosity, support and assistance in the creation of my books and writing career.

To my gorgeous parents, Rosanna and Michael, for their unconditional love, generosity, support and belief and so much more!

To family and friends for their love, encouragement and sharing in my joy. To one and all THANK YOU.

About the Author

Kristina is a children's book author who is passionate about children's literacy and education. She holds a Diploma of Teaching (Primary), Bachelor of Education (Primary) and a Masters of Education (Teaching English to Speakers of Other Languages). She is the author of eight children's books.

Kristina has taught at a number of primary schools and universities. She currently works part-time at RMIT University as an Academic Skills Advisor.

She lives in Melbourne Australia with her husband and two daughters. Kristina has always loved to write and spends many hours writing reading, watching and listening for ideas. She carries a small notebook and pen with her to 'catch' ideas before they evaporate. Her wonderful ideas can come from anywhere at any time!

Lightning Source UK Ltd.
Milton Keynes UK
UKHW051255190720
366743UK00002B/43

* 9 7 8 0 6 4 8 7 0 7 2 6 4 *